Mouse Shapes

Ellen Stoll Walsh

Harcourt, Inc.

Orlando   Austin   New York   San Diego   Toronto   London

Requests for permission to make copies of any part of the work should be submitted online at www.harcourt.com/contact or mailed to the following address:
Permissions Department, Harcourt, Inc., 6277 Sea Harbor Drive, Orlando, Florida 32887-6777.

www.HarcourtBooks.com

Library of Congress Cataloging-in-Publication Data
Walsh, Ellen Stoll.
Mouse shapes/Ellen Stoll Walsh.
p. cm.
Summary:Three mice make a variety of things out of different shapes
as they hide from a scary cat.
[1.Shape—Fiction. 2.Mice—Fiction.] I.Title.
PZ7.W1675Mou 2007
[E]—dc22   2006013695
ISBN 978-0-15-206091-6

H G F E D C B

Printed in Singapore

The illustrations in this book are cut-paper collage.
The display and text type was set in ITC Modern.
Color separations by Colourscan Co. Pte. Ltd., Singapore
Printed and bound by Tien Wah Press, Singapore
This book was printed on totally chlorine-free Stora Enso Matte paper.
Production supervision by Christine Witnik
Designed by Lauren Rille

For Betsy and Ron

The mice were running from the cat.
"Hurry!" said Violet.

"Let's hide in here," said Martin.

After a while, Fred said, "I think we lost him."

"Look, we've been hiding in shapes!" said Violet.

"We can make things with them. Here's a square. A triangle on top makes it a perfect house for a little mouse."

"A triangle and a rectangle make a tree,"
said Martin. "This circle is the sun."

"But these triangles are different," said Fred.
"Triangles are tricky," said Violet. "But any
shape with three sides is a triangle."

Fred put two circles on a rectangle. "It's a wagon for the little mouse in the house," he said.

"Two diamonds make a book for
the little mouse to read," said Violet.

"Here's one oval, two circles, and eight triangles,"
said Martin. "It's a fish!"

"Watch out—the cat likes fish," said Violet.

"Hey, let's make the cat!" said Fred.
Violet put on the eyes and nose.
Fred stuck on the ears.

And Martin added the teeth.

"It looks just like the real cat," he said.

"Only better."

Just then the real cat pounced.

The mice ran away...

and didn't come back until the cat was gone.

"That cat's too sneaky," said Violet. "If only we were bigger."

"I have an idea!" said Fred.

The clever mice got to work.

Soon they made three big scary mice . . .

and surprised the cat!

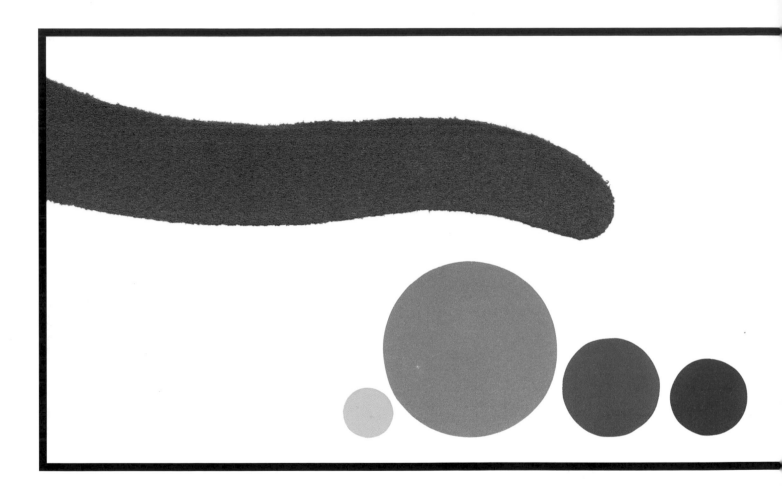

The cat ran away, fast.
"What a scaredy-cat," said Violet. "Now what
can we make for the little mouse in the house?"

"It's time for lunch," said Fred. "Let's
make him some Swiss cheese."

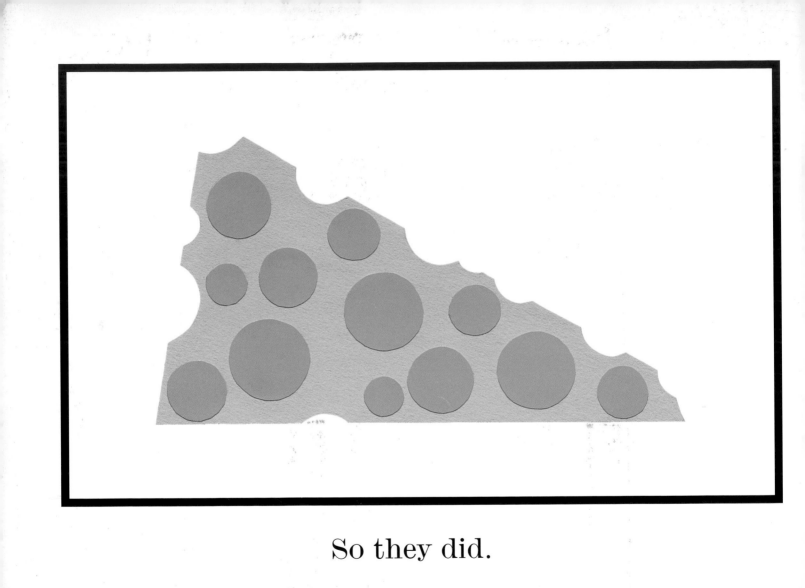

So they did.

BT
7/07

E   Walsh, Ellen Stoll.

     Mouse shapes.